254

WHITE BIRD

WEEKLY READER
CHILDREN'S BOOK CLUB

WEEKLY READER CHILDREN'S BOOK CLUB

presents

Clyde Robert Bulla

WHITE BIRD

ILLUSTRATED BY

Leonard Weisgard

THOMAS Y. CROWELL COMPANY   NEW YORK

To Robert L. Crowell

Designed by JOAN MAESTRO

MANUFACTURED IN THE UNITED STATES OF AMERICA

Library of Congress Catalog Card No. AC 66-10505

Weekly Reader Book Club Edition

By the Author

The Donkey Cart
Riding the Pony Express
The Secret Valley
Surprise for a Cowboy
A Ranch for Danny
Johnny Hong of Chinatown
Song of St. Francis
Eagle Feather
Star of Wild Horse Canyon
Down the Mississippi
Squanto, Friend of the
    White Men
The Poppy Seeds
White Sails to China
The Sword in the Tree
John Billington, Friend
    of Squanto
Old Charlie

Ghost Town Treasure
Pirate's Promise
Stories of Favorite Operas
The Valentine Cat
Three-Dollar Mule
A Tree Is a Plant
The Sugar Pear Tree
Benito
The Ring and the Fire
What Makes a Shadow?
Viking Adventure
Indian Hill
St. Valentine's Day
More Stories of Favorite
    Operas
Lincoln's Birthday
White Bird

Contents

Chapter 1

John Thomas

n the spring of 1785 Andrew Vail and his family left their home in Virginia. Three other families went with them. On horseback and in wagons they crossed the mountains into Tennessee.

Andrew Vail was their leader. He was tough and strong as an old tree. His eyes flashed when he was angry. His wife and son had always obeyed him. The rest of the band obeyed him, too.

They came to Half-Moon Valley, where no white man had ever lived before. Andrew Vail liked the woods and the river. He liked the high hills that seemed to shut out the rest of the world. "This will be our home," he said, and no one dared to speak against him.

They built log cabins, four in a row. They began to farm the half-moon of land between the river and the hills. "Here we can be happy," said Andrew Vail. "Here we can build a world of our own—better than the world we left behind."

But not everyone was happy in Half-Moon Valley.

"This land is poor and full of rocks," said one of the men.

"And the river floods the best part of it," said another. "We can find better farms somewhere else."

Andrew Vail was angry. "If an easy life is all you want," he said, "go and find it."

The men talked among themselves. Then they took their wives and went away to look for better land.

Only two families were left in the valley—the three Vails and Will Barlow and his wife, Hannah. Sometimes the Barlows wished they had gone with the others. "But Andrew and his wife were our neighbors back in Virginia," said Hannah. "It's hard to leave such old friends."

So they stayed, and the years passed. More people came over the mountains. By the hundreds they built their houses on the good land. None of them stopped in Half-Moon Valley.

Andrew Vail and his wife grew old. They both died in the same year.

Their son, Luke, stayed on in the cabin. He had always been a quiet man who worked hard and said little. Now he worked harder and said even less.

Will and Hannah Barlow used to watch him as he cut wood, made fences, and grew his poor crops. "Work, work," they would say. "That's all he knows."

Then came the day that changed Luke's life.

There had been a storm the night before. In the morning Luke was up early, looking over his fields. The rain had washed out most of his young corn.

He looked toward the river and listened to its roar. Part of the valley was flooded. A log had floated into the tall, green cane that grew along the river. And something had washed up against the

log, something that looked like a box or a little boat.

Luke went toward it. It was not a box or a boat, but something he had not seen in many a year.

It was a baby's cradle.

He waded through the water. He bent over the cradle. There was a pink quilt inside it, and something moved under the quilt. Something cried in a voice like the mewing of a kitten.

He drew back the quilt. A baby looked up at him—a crying baby with a round, red face.

He picked up the cradle. He began to run, splashing the water as he went. He ran all the way to the Barlows' cabin.

Hannah came to the door. "What on earth!" she cried.

"It's a baby," said Luke. "It's a little baby!"

He carried the cradle inside and put it down. Hannah fell on her knees beside it. "Mercy on us!" she said. She picked up the baby. "Oh, he's so cold!" she said.

Will Barlow came in. He looked at the baby, then at his wife. He tried to speak, but all he could say was "What—what—?"

"The baby was in the cradle," Luke told him. "The cradle was out there in the water. It must have come down the river."

Hannah wrapped the baby in an old shirt. He put up his hands and pulled at her dress. "Poor little soul, he's hungry." She said to Will, "Take him while I warm some milk."

"I'll take him," said Luke. Very carefully he set the baby on his knee.

"Whose baby is it?" asked Will.

"We don't know," said Luke.

"Maybe there's something here that tells." Will was looking inside the cradle. "Here's something carved in the wood."

"What is it?" asked Hannah.

"It's two letters," said Will. "J and T."

"That must be for the baby's name," said Luke.

"Maybe J is for John and T is for—I don't know. Maybe Thomas."

Hannah brought warm milk in a pan. She tried to feed the baby with a spoon.

"He doesn't know how to eat this way," said Luke.

"How else are we going to feed him?" said Hannah. "Here, baby. Here, little John Thomas. Open your mouth."

At the end of half an hour the baby was fed. "More milk went outside than inside," said Hannah, "but he's quiet now."

The baby looked about him. He looked longest at the firelight on the wall.

"Oh, I wish you could talk!" said Hannah. "Then you could tell us who you are and where you came from."

"Maybe he *can* talk," said Will.

"No, he's too little," said Hannah. "He can't be more than eight months old."

"He looks older to me," said Will.

"He's young enough to need his mother," said Hannah, "and I hope she comes looking for him soon."

Chapter 2

Behind the Rocks

week went by, and no one had
come looking for the baby.

"It isn't right to wait any longer," said Hannah.
"We have to find out where he belongs."

Will saddled a horse and rode away.

The next day he was back. He had talked with
people who lived along the river. They had told
him of a man and woman who came down the old
Indian trail in a wagon. No one knew their names
or where they were from. The woman had blue
eyes and yellow hair, and she had a baby who
looked like her. On the day of the storm they
stopped at a farm. The man said he wanted to cross

7

the river, and they drove away. No one saw them after that.

"The baby must have been John Thomas," said Hannah.

"Yes," said Will, "and the flood must have caught those people and carried them away— horses, wagon, and all."

"Oh, don't say that!" said Hannah.

"Maybe John Thomas was in his cradle in the back of the wagon," said Will. "Maybe when the wagon sank, the cradle floated out."

"Those poor people—I hope and pray they *weren't* lost in the flood," said Hannah. "Wouldn't it be wonderful if they came here, looking for the baby? Then we could say, 'Here he is,' and they could all be happy together again."

But weeks passed, and months, and no one came looking for John Thomas.

By the end of summer he could walk and talk. He had grown too big for his cradle.

That winter he stayed most of the time in Luke's cabin.

"It's a good thing for Luke," said Hannah. "It's company for him. It gives him someone to talk to, and he does take good care of the baby."

Luke cooked corn meal mush, and John Thomas ate it with milk and wild honey. In the winter the hens laid only a few eggs, but whenever there was an egg, Luke cooked it for John Thomas.

Luke made him deerskin moccasins. Hannah made him a deerskin suit.

"Such a fine boy," she said. "It's a pity he has no other child to play with."

"He won't miss what he never had," said Luke.

"Just the same, it isn't right," said Hannah, and she shook her head. "Oh, this is a lonesome place."

The summer came when John Thomas was four years old. At least, Luke and Will and Hannah thought he must be four. They had no way of being sure. That was the summer when George and Jenny Barlow came to the valley.

George and Jenny were cousins of Will and Hannah. One day the four Barlows came to Luke's cabin. Will and Hannah were excited.

"George and Jenny are leaving soon," said Hannah, "and we're going with them."

"It's been a hard life, trying to farm the land here," said Will. "We should have left long ago."

"We're going to the Mississippi Valley," said Cousin George. "Most of the Indians are west of the Mississippi River now, and there's no danger from them. There's good land waiting, and you don't have to break your back to make a living."

"Will and I are too old to work like young people," said Hannah, "and so are you, Luke. Come and go with us."

Luke said, "This was my father and mother's home. It's my home, too, and I'll not leave it."

"We don't want to go without you," said Will.

"I told you," Luke said, "I'm not going."

"But you'll be all alone," said Hannah. "What will you do without us and John Thomas?"

"John Thomas?" said Luke. "He's staying with me."

"Oh, no!" said Hannah.

"Oh, yes," said Luke.

"What would become of him in this lonely place?" said Hannah. "You can't keep him here."

"I found him. I saved him from the river," said Luke. "It's for me to say whether he goes or stays."

"Hannah," said Will, "he may be right."

"I won't have it," she said. "I just won't have it. John Thomas is going with us!"

By the next evening the Barlows were ready to leave. The two wagons were loaded. The horses were tied outside the cabin. The cattle were in the pen, waiting to be driven away.

John Thomas slept in Luke's cabin that night. In the morning, before the sun was up, Luke took the boy from his bed. He dressed him and carried him outside.

John Thomas was half asleep. "Where are we going?" he asked.

"You'll see," said Luke.

He carried the boy into the woods.

"I can walk," said John Thomas.

Luke put him down. They walked through the woods and up a hill. They stopped in a hollow behind two big rocks.

The sun came up. Luke and John Thomas could look from behind the rocks and see down into the valley. They could see the Barlows' cabin and the people out in front.

One of the women went to Luke's cabin. One of the men went to the edge of the woods. Someone called Luke's name, then John Thomas'.

John Thomas started to climb out over the rocks.

Luke pulled him back. "Don't let them see see you," he said.

The sun rose high. The Barlows were still moving about in front of the cabin, as if they were not sure what to do. But at last they got into the wagons. The wagons began to move. Slowly they moved up the old trail and out of sight beyond the hills.

Chapter 3

A Raft on the River

ay after day John Thomas went to the Barlows' cabin to look for Will and Hannah.

"Are they coming back tomorrow?" he would ask.

"I don't think so," Luke would say.

And after a while John Thomas stopped asking about them. He almost forgot they had ever lived there.

Every day he followed Luke.

Luke talked to him and sometimes told him stories. All the stories were from the Bible.

"Did Moses live here?" asked John Thomas. "Did David live here?"

"No, they lived across the sea," said Luke.

14

"What is the sea?" asked John Thomas.

"It's water. It's so much water that you wouldn't believe it," said Luke. "People sail across it in big boats."

"How big?" asked John Thomas. "As big as this house?"

"Bigger," said Luke.

"I want to sail in one of them," said John Thomas.

"Well, you can't," said Luke. "The sea is too far off."

As John Thomas grew older, he helped Luke more and more. He worked in the fields and garden. He carried water from the spring. He cut wood and brought it to the house.

"You're quick to learn things," Luke told him. "A big boy like you, you could learn your numbers if you put your head to it."

He taught John Thomas to count. He tried to teach him to read.

John Thomas looked into the big, black Bible. He asked, "Is this the only book there is?"

"It's the only one I'll have in *my* house," said Luke. "You'll read that or nothing."

It took a long time, but John Thomas learned to read the Bible. He learned a little writing, too. He wrote with charcoal on a piece of board. When the board was covered, he washed it off with soap and water and used it again.

Luke said one day, "Now you know as much as if you'd been to school."

"Did you ever go to school?" asked John Thomas.

"No. My father taught me all I needed to know," said Luke, "and I can teach you all you need to know."

John Thomas liked the cold winter days when he and Luke were together by the fire. But even more he liked the days when he could be outside. Sometimes he walked in the woods. Sometimes he went to the river to fish or throw rocks into the water.

Once he saw a raft go by. A man, a boy, and a dog were on the raft.

The boy waved. John Thomas waved back. He watched until the raft was out of sight. Then he ran to the cabin to find Luke.

"Did you see the raft?" he asked. "There was a
boy on it. He waved at me."

"Did you wave at him?" asked Luke.

"Yes," said John Thomas.

"Don't ever do it again," said Luke. "The next
time you see anybody, you hide in the bushes."

"Why?" asked John Thomas.

"Because people like that might make trouble for us," said Luke. "We're better off by ourselves."

"The boy had a dog," said John Thomas. "Could I have a dog?"

"That's what I mean," said Luke. "Those people didn't even stop, but still they made trouble. They made you want something you can't have."

"Could I have a dog if I found one?" asked John Thomas.

"You won't be finding a dog here," said Luke. "Get to work now. And give thanks for what you have instead of wanting more."

Chapter 4

The Peddler-Man

ohn Thomas worked hardest in the fall. He and Luke cut wood for the fireplace. They picked corn. They dug potatoes and put them away in the cellar along with the onions, pumpkins, and squashes. They gathered nuts.

On a day in fall John Thomas went to the woods to look for nuts. He found a hickory tree. With a long stick he began to knock down the nuts that grew among the yellow leaves.

Something ran through the bushes in front of him. It might be a wolf, he thought. It might be a bear.

He stood watching.

The animal came out into the open.

Luke had said, "You won't be finding a dog here." But here was one—a short-legged, brown dog with a wagging tail!

"Here," said John Thomas. "Come here."

The dog growled, but his tail kept wagging.

John Thomas went toward him. Then he stopped. A man had come out of the woods.

He was like no one John Thomas had ever seen before. His clothes were of dark homespun. His cheeks were round and pink, and his thick, dark hair had gray in it. He was smiling.

The dog went to him.

The man spoke to John Thomas, "Don't be afraid of Jip. He won't hurt you."

"I'm not afraid," said John Thomas.

"Jip ran after a rabbit. I ran after Jip, and now we're lost," said the man. "Where is the trail?"

"Which trail?" asked John Thomas.

"The one along the river," said the man. "The one that leads to town."

"The river runs out of the valley through those high cliffs," said John Thomas. "There's nowhere to walk between them. You have to go over the hills to get to the river trail."

"And where am I now?" asked the man.

"In Half-Moon Valley," John Thomas told him.

"Ah," said the man. "Then you must be the boy who came down the river in his cradle."

"How did you know?" asked John Thomas.

"People talk about such things," said the man. "I heard about you when I first came to Tennessee, and that was many years ago. How old are you now?"

"Luke says I'm eleven," said John Thomas.

"Luke," said the man. "That's Luke Vail, isn't it?"

"Do you know him?" asked John Thomas.

"I've only heard of him," said the man, "the same as I've heard of you."

"If you don't know him, you'd better go," said John Thomas. "He doesn't want any strangers here."

"Cross is my name—Sam Cross," said the man. "People call me the peddler-man. I come through the country with things to sell. Pots and pans, needles and thread, cotton and linen—whatever you need. So now you know me. So now I'm not a stranger." He smiled.

John Thomas did not smile back. "You'd better go," he said.

"All right," said the man. "But first will you show me where to water my horse?"

"I don't see any horse," said John Thomas.

The man led the way to where a gray pony was tied to a tree. There was a saddle on the pony. Behind the saddle was a large pack covered with cloth.

"There's a spring on the other side of these rocks," said John Thomas. "I'll show you."

They went to the spring. Water ran out of a bank and into a round pool. The pony drank. Sam Cross drank, too.

Jip wanted to play. He ran back and forth through the leaves that had fallen. He ran to John Thomas and licked him under the chin. His tongue tickled, and John Thomas laughed.

"Jip is only two years old. He still thinks he's a puppy," said the peddler. "Do you have a dog?"

"No," said John Thomas. "Once I wanted one, but I never got it."

"Do you still want one?" asked Sam.

"Yes," said John Thomas.

"Some friends of mine have six puppies," said Sam. "You could have one if you went after it."

"Where are they?" asked John Thomas.

"In town," said Sam.

"I couldn't go there," said John Thomas.

"Why not?" asked Sam.

"Luke says I'm better off not to go," said John Thomas. "He says the way the world is, I'm better off to stay here."

"Don't you ever go to town?" asked Sam.

"Well—Luke goes once in a while," said John Thomas.

"But you don't go?" asked Sam.

John Thomas shook his head.

Sam asked him, "Haven't you ever gone outside this valley?"

"I've *looked* outside," said John Thomas. "I've been to the top of the hill and looked over."

A rifle shot sounded in the woods not far away.

"That's Luke. He's hunting, and he might come this way," said John Thomas. "You'd better go."

"All right." Sam held out his hand.

John Thomas looked at it.

"Won't you shake hands with me?" asked Sam.

" 'Shake hands'?" said John Thomas. "What is that?"

Sam took hold of John Thomas' hand and shook it.

"What is that for?" asked John Thomas.

"It's something people do when they meet or say good-by," said Sam. He got on his pony and rode away. Jip ran after the pony.

There was another rifle shot, nearer than before.

John Thomas went back to the hickory tree. He began to fill his sack with hickory nuts. He worked fast, trying to make up for the time he had lost.

Chapter 5

Strange Spring

ll the rest of the day John Thomas
thought about the puppies in town. He woke up
in the night and thought about them.

At breakfast the next morning he asked Luke,
"When are you going to town again?"

"Not till I have to," said Luke. "It takes a whole
day."

"When you go," said John Thomas, "could I go
with you?"

Luke gave him a sharp look. "What for?"

"Just—just to see," said John Thomas.

"It's no place for you," said Luke. "I keep telling you the world out there is so full of bad people you just wouldn't believe it. I'd never go near that hateful town if we didn't need salt or rope or nails sometimes."

"Do they have dogs in town?" asked John Thomas.

"Dogs all over the place, barking and biting," said Luke. "Why?"

"I was thinking," said John Thomas, "that somebody might have one to give away. I was thinking that somebody might have a puppy—"

"Is that what you want—a puppy?" asked Luke.

"Yes," said John Thomas.

"Well, you can't have it," said Luke. "We don't need a dog. And if you did have one, you'd get foolish over it. Then it would die or get lost, and you'd feel worse than you did before." He was looking at John Thomas. "What put this idea in your head all of a sudden?"

"It isn't all of a sudden," said John Thomas. "A long time ago I was thinking—"

"Well, you can stop thinking," said Luke. "You can stop right now."

But John Thomas kept thinking about the puppies in town. All through the winter he thought about the one that might be his. By the time spring came, he knew the puppy was grown and would never belong to him.

That was a strange spring. There were storms and floods. There were gray skies and cold rains. Luke and John Thomas waited for the rains to stop so they could plant the fields and garden.

John Thomas grew tired of staying inside. He went out into the rain. He had made himself a rabbit-skin cap, and he wore it to keep his head dry.

Sometimes he walked past the three empty cabins. They were covered with vines, and there were snakes and spiders inside.

Sometimes he walked in the woods. The branches were almost like a roof over his head.

One day after a storm he went out into the woods. He came upon a great oak tree that had been struck by lightning. The trunk was burned and split. Sticks and leaves were scattered about on the ground. And there was something else on the ground—something white that was almost hidden in the grass.

At first John Thomas thought it was a flower or
a toadstool. Then he saw that it was a bird.

It lay very still. John Thomas wondered if it had
been in the tree when the lightning struck.

He went toward the bird. It moved. It flopped a
little way in the wet grass, then lay still again.

He picked it up. He could feel its heart beat. It
opened one eye for a moment. The eye was pink.

The white bird was the size of a half-grown
crow. It had the head and shape of a crow.

But crows were black.

John Thomas took the bird back to the cabin.

"What have you got there?" asked Luke. He looked at the bird. He spread out one of its wings.

"What do you think it is?" asked John Thomas.

"It's a crow," said Luke.

"How can it be?" asked John Thomas. "It's white all over."

"Once in a while this happens," said Luke. "An animal is born all white. When I was a boy I saw a squirrel that was white with pink eyes. But I never saw a white crow before."

"It's hurt," said John Thomas. "There's blood on its wing."

"It won't live," said Luke. "Get rid of it."

John Thomas took the bird outside. He started to put it down on the ground. But the ground was wet and cold.

He took the bird to the woodshed. Inside he found a dry spot in a corner. He left the bird there.

Chapter 6

The Cage

n the morning John Thomas went to the woodshed. The bird was nowhere in sight.

He looked about the shed. He looked behind the pile of wood. There sat the bird.

John Thomas touched its feathers. The bird gave a little squawk.

John Thomas ran back to the cabin. He asked Luke, "What do you feed a crow?"

"That bird you had yesterday?" asked Luke.

"Yes," said John Thomas.

"You don't feed it anything," said Luke. "You turn it loose."

"It can't fly," said John Thomas. "I have to take care of it till it can fly."

"Why do you?" asked Luke.

"Because I brought it here," said John Thomas, "and it can't take care of itself."

"I'll not have that bird in the house," said Luke. "Ugly thing!"

"I won't bring it in, Luke," said John Thomas. He filled a dish with water and took it to the woodshed. Later, when Luke was out of the cabin, he took the crow some bread.

He picked up the bird. He opened its beak very gently and fed it a bite of bread soaked in water.

"Krawk!" went the bird, and opened its mouth for more.

John Thomas fed it the rest of the bread. Then the bird flopped off his knee and hid again behind the wood.

Before many days John Thomas did not have to put the food into the bird's mouth. The bird ate from the dish and picked up the cracked corn that John Thomas threw down before it.

"You've had that bird a week," said Luke. "Turn it loose."

"It isn't well yet," said John Thomas.

"No, and it won't get well, shut up in that old dark shed," said Luke. "Turn it loose, I tell you."

John Thomas sat in the shed with the crow. The door was open just enough to let in a little light. The crow hopped over into the light.

"I know you want out, White Bird," said John Thomas, "but I can't turn you loose. There are too many things waiting to catch you. There are foxes and weasels and snakes, and you can't fly away from them."

He tried to think what to do. An idea came to him.

He went to the willow trees that grew along the river. He brought back an armload of willow branches. He wove them together into a long, loose basket. At the top he tied the branches together with string.

Luke said, "That's a bird cage. How did you know how to make a bird cage?"

"I don't know," said John Thomas. "It was just an idea I had."

He put the bird into the cage.

"This is your house, White Bird," he said.

He hung the cage in a tree. He hung it so that
the crow would have both sun and shade. At night
he took the bird to the woodshed.

He liked to talk to the bird and stroke its feathers. White Bird grew tame. Sometimes it made a
clucking sound when John Thomas came near.

One day John Thomas had set the cage by the
cabin. He was lying on the grass; talking to the
crow.

"Shall I bring you worms?" he said. "Shall I
bring you a big red berry?"

The crow put its head on one side as if it were listening.

"Do you know what I'm saying?" said John Thomas. "Do you know just a little of what I'm saying?"

The crow blinked its eyes. John Thomas laughed. Then he jumped to his feet. Luke was there. Luke was saying, "I called you. Why don't you speak up when I call you?"

"I didn't hear you," said John Thomas.

"I heard *you,*" said Luke. "Talking to that bird, when there's work to be done. Talking to that bird, so you can't hear when I call you!"

He opened the cage door. He reached inside.

"Don't!" said John Thomas.

Luke had hold of the bird. He pulled it out of the cage and threw it into the air.

"It can't fly!" said John Thomas.

"It *can* fly," said Luke. "Leave it alone."

But John Thomas went running after the bird. It flew a little way and fell. Half hopping, half flying, it disappeared into the bushes.

John Thomas crawled after it. Luke caught him by the leg and dragged him out.

"No, I've got to find White Bird!" said John Thomas.

"Leave it alone, I tell you," said Luke. "Get on up to the spring. Bring back a bucket of water before dark."

John Thomas went to the spring. He brought back a bucket of water. By that time the sun was down. He knew he could not find the bird in the dark.

He hardly slept that night. As soon as daylight came, he went outside. He went toward the place where he had last seen the bird.

A sound came to him: "Krawk!"

He stopped. The cage was still by the side of the cabin. And inside the cage was White Bird!

Luke came out of the cabin. "That fool crow!" he said. "It doesn't have sense enough to fly away."

"It knows its wing isn't well yet," said John Thomas. "That's why it came back."

"What if its wing never gets well?" asked Luke.

John Thomas did not answer, but he said to himself, then I'll always keep it and take care of it.

Chapter 7

Two Men and a Boy

he warm days of summer had come. The corn was as high as John Thomas' head. The weeds were high, too, and he and Luke hoed them out of the fields.

Late one afternoon they hung their hoes on the fence. They went to the river to wash before supper. When they started to the cabin, they saw three strangers coming toward them.

The strangers were two men and a boy. The men had long faces and straggling beards. The boy was tall and thin. His eyes were pale. His mouth hung open a little.

One of the men spoke. "I'm Fred Tripp. These are my brothers, Ernie and Tad. We came to look for land to buy."

"There's none here that you'd want," said Luke.

"We found that out," said the man. "Tomorrow we'll be getting on to town."

Luke said to John Thomas, "Come." They went on toward the cabin. The three brothers followed. Tad, the youngest, caught up with John Thomas and began to ask questions. "Who lives here? Just you and your father?"

"He isn't my father," said John Thomas.

"Oh," said Tad. "Are you going to give us something to eat?"

"I don't know," said John Thomas.

Tad saw the cage in a tree beside the cabin. "What's that?" he asked.

"A cage," said John Thomas.

"What's in it?" Tad went closer. "It's a bird. It looks like a white crow. Is that what it is? A white crow?"

"Yes," said John Thomas.

"I never saw such a thing before," said Tad. "Look at its eyes, like little red lamps! Oh, you're

a pretty bird!" He reached into the cage and tried
to feel the bird's feathers.

"Don't hurt it," said John Thomas.

"Oh, I wouldn't hurt it. I never saw such a
pretty bird before," said Tad. "What's its name?"

"I call it White Bird," said John Thomas.

"That's not much of a name. I'd give it a better
one if I had it." Tad was looking into the cage. "I
want this bird. Give it to me."

"No!" said John Thomas.

"Look." Tad showed him a knife. "I'll trade
you this for it."

John Thomas shook his head. He took the bird
out of the cage.

"What are you going to do with it?" asked Tad.

"Put it in the woodshed," said John Thomas.
"That's where it stays at night."

"I've got a chain. It's part gold," said Tad. "I'll
trade you the chain and the knife, too."

"No," said John Thomas. He took the bird to
the woodshed.

Fred Tripp was talking with Luke. "We'll be
staying all night," he said. "Is there room for us in
your house?"

"There's more room outside," said Luke.

"You're not very friendly," said Fred.

"Nobody ever said I was," said Luke.

He and John Thomas went into the cabin, and Luke shut the door.

It was hard for John Thomas to go to sleep that night. He lay awake and listened to the sounds outside. He heard the wind. He heard an owl cry. Once he thought he heard someone talking.

When he woke in the morning, Luke was up and dressed.

"Where are the people?" asked John Thomas.

"Gone," said Luke. "They left about daylight."

John Thomas went out to feed and water his bird. The woodshed door was open. He was sure he had left it shut.

He looked inside the shed. "White Bird?" he said. He looked behind the wood. The bird was gone.

"Luke!" he called.

Luke came out of the cabin.

"My bird is gone," said John Thomas. "The door was open. You didn't open it, did you?"

"No," said Luke.

"Then *he* turned it loose," said John Thomas. "That boy wanted White Bird, and I wouldn't give it to him. Maybe—maybe he *took* it!"

Luke said nothing.

"If he took my bird, I'll get it back," said John Thomas. "I'll go after him and—"

"I'm going to tell you something," said Luke. "The boy did take the bird. I saw him take it and put it under his coat."

"You *saw* him?" said John Thomas. "You let him take it, and you didn't tell me?"

"No, I didn't, and I'll tell you why," said Luke. "Every day I saw you and that crow together. I heard you talking to it and making a fool of yourself. When I saw that boy take the bird, I knew it was the best thing for everybody."

John Thomas started away.

"Where are you going?" asked Luke.

"I'm going after them," said John Thomas.

"Come back here." Luke caught John Thomas' arm.

John Thomas broke away.

Again Luke caught him. John Thomas fought. He shouted, "Let me go!"

Luke dragged him to the woodshed. He pushed him inside and shut the door.

John Thomas threw himself against the door. It would not open. Luke had propped it shut from the outside.

Chapter 8

In the Night

ohn Thomas sat in the dark shed. Over and over he thought, Tad took my bird. He may forget to water it. He may forget to feed it. My bird will die.

He found a log that had been cut for the fireplace. He picked it up and beat on the door with it. The walls shook, but the door did not open or break.

John Thomas sat down again. After a long time he heard steps outside. The door opened. Luke said, "You can come out now."

John Thomas went out into the light.

"Go eat your breakfast," said Luke.

43

John Thomas did not move.

Luke gave him a push. "Go on," he said.

Inside the cabin, John Thomas found breakfast on the table—a corn cake and a piece of cold bacon. He could not eat. His throat was too dry.

"Come out when you're through," said Luke.

John Thomas went outside.

"Here is your hoe," said Luke.

John Thomas took his hoe and began to hoe the weeds out of the corn. Luke worked beside him.

They came to the end of the cornfield. John Thomas put down his hoe.

"What's the matter?" asked Luke.

"I want a drink," said John Thomas. He was on his way toward the woods.

"Where are you going?" asked Luke.

"To the spring," said John Thomas.

"There's water in the cabin," said Luke.

"I want it cold out of the spring," said John Thomas.

"You'll take it out of the bucket," said Luke.

John Thomas went into the cabin. With the gourd dipper he dipped some water out of the bucket. He drank a little. It was warm. The taste of it made him feel sick. He went back to the field.

He and Luke worked most of the day. All the time Luke watched John Thomas and kept close to him.

After supper they sat in the cabin. Luke lighted a candle, opened the Bible, and began to read aloud. At the end of a page he said, "You're not listening."

"Yes, I am," said John Thomas.

"No, you're not," said Luke. "You're thinking about that bird."

John Thomas said nothing.

"That bird was no good for you," said Luke. "What I did was right. Some day you'll *see* I was right."

Still John Thomas said nothing. He did not want to talk to Luke. He did not even want to look at him.

He went to bed and turned his face away from the light.

Luke blew out the candle and went to bed on the other side of the room.

John Thomas lay still. He waited until he thought Luke must be asleep. He got out of bed.

He felt for his clothes and put them on. Very softly he walked across the room.

A chair was in his way. He bumped into it. He heard Luke move in bed.

"John Thomas?" said Luke. "Is that you?"

John Thomas was at the door. He threw it open. He ran out into the night.

Luke was shouting, "Come back here!"

John Thomas ran on. He ran until the cabin was far behind him. In the darkness he could see only a little way before him, but he knew the path up the hill. He came to the top and started down the other side.

Chapter 9

Joe Roddy's Store

eyond the hilltop John Thomas did not know his way in the dark. He stood under a tree, catching his breath and listening. He heard the cries of birds and the footsteps of small animals. A wolf howled a long way off.

John Thomas climbed the tree. He felt safe there. He sat on a large branch and put his head against the tree trunk. After a long time he went to sleep.

He woke early. There was light in the sky, and he could see his way through the woods. He found a path and followed it to the river. From there the trail ran beside the river all the way to town. This was what he had heard Luke say.

As he walked along the trail, he looked at the tracks in the dust. Some had been made by horses and wagons. Others had been made by people on foot. Some of the tracks might have been made by the Tripp brothers, he thought.

He walked faster. He walked past one farm, then another.

A man came along on horseback. "Are you headed for town?" he asked.

"Yes," said John Thomas.

"So am I," said the man. "Climb on."

He put out a hand and swung John Thomas up behind him.

They rode until the middle of the day.

"Is it much farther?" asked John Thomas.

"No," said the man.

John Thomas began to see roofs ahead, the roofs of many houses close together. He saw a large wheel that turned and splashed in the river. He pointed. "What is that?"

"That's a mill," said the man.

"What is it for?" asked John Thomas.

"It grinds the grain," said the man. "Didn't you ever see a mill before?"

"No," said John Thomas. He pointed to a house with a high peak on the roof. "What is that?"

"That's a church," said the man. "Didn't you ever see a church before?"

"I never came to town before," said John Thomas.

"Where have you been?" asked the man.

"In Half-Moon Valley," said John Thomas.

"What brings you here now?" asked the man.

John Thomas told him about his bird and the Tripp brothers. "I have to find them and get my bird back," he said. "But with all these houses, I don't know where to look."

"I'll put you off at Joe Roddy's store," said the man. "You ask in there."

Joe Roddy's store was a log cabin on the edge of town. John Thomas went inside. He saw shelves and tables piled with cloth and clothing, dishes and pans. He saw barrels of flour and salt.

A man came out of the back of the store. He was a neat-looking man in a blue-striped shirt. "What can I do for you?" he asked.

John Thomas asked, "Are you Joe Roddy?"

"That's my name," said the man.

"Do you know the Tripp brothers?" asked John Thomas.

"Never heard of them," said the man.

"They are two men and a boy," said John Thomas.

"Two men and a boy came here yesterday," said Joe Roddy. "The boy had a bird—"

"A white bird?" asked John Thomas.

"Yes," said Joe Roddy. "A white bird. The oddest bird I ever saw. It looked like a crow, yet it was all white."

"It's mine," said John Thomas. "I have to get it back."

"You mean they stole it from you?" asked Joe Roddy.

"Yes," said John Thomas. "They came through Half-Moon Valley and—"

"Half-Moon Valley?" said Joe. "Then you must be Luke Vail's boy."

"I'm not his boy," said John Thomas.

"You live with him, don't you?" asked Joe.

"I did live with him," said John Thomas.

"Where did the Tripp brothers go? I have to find them."

"They took the north road out of town," said Joe. "That was yesterday. They said they were looking for land to buy. I heard one of them say they might come back through town today."

"Would they be coming to your store again?" asked John Thomas.

"They might be," said Joe.

"Then could I wait for them here?" asked John Thomas.

Two women came into the store.

Joe told John Thomas, "Sit down in the back. I'll talk to you in a minute."

John Thomas sat down on a bench.

As soon as the women were gone, Joe came to the back of the store. He asked John Thomas, "How about a bite to eat?"

John Thomas only looked at him.

"Aren't you hungry?" asked Joe.

"In a store you have to have money or something to trade, don't you?" said John Thomas. "I don't have anything."

"You can pay me later." Joe brought him some

bread and cheese and a sour pickle. He went away while John Thomas ate.

The rest of the day John Thomas sat in the store.

Evening came. The Tripp brothers had not come.

"I'd better go out looking for them," he said.

"Where would you look?" asked Joe.

"Didn't you say they went up the north road?" asked John Thomas.

"Yes, but it's too late to start out now," said Joe. "Stay here tonight, and in the morning you'd better go home."

"I have to find them," said John Thomas.

Joe closed the store. He brought a blanket and spread it on the floor. John Thomas slept there that night.

Chapter 10

Isabel

n the morning John Thomas had breakfast with Joe Roddy.

"Why don't you go home now?" asked Joe. "You might have to walk all over Tennessee before you catch up with the Tripp brothers."

"I have to find them," said John Thomas.

He said good-by to Joe. He took the north road out of town.

For most of the morning he walked, past woods and pastures, past fields and houses.

Then the road became two roads. He did not know which to take.

Back among the trees he saw a house with a high

stone chimney. He thought the people who lived there might have seen the Tripp brothers.

As he turned in at the lane that led to the house, three dogs rushed toward him. They were yelping and showing their teeth.

John Thomas ran for the nearest tree. There was a ditch in his way. He fell into it. He went splashing into mud and water up to his knees.

He climbed out. The dogs were nearly upon him. He ran to the tree. He jumped, caught a low branch, and pulled himself up.

The dogs ran back and forth below. They put their paws on the tree and looked up at him. Their barking was fierce and ugly.

A tall black man came out of the house and up the lane. "Who's there?" he asked.

A girl ran behind him. She was slim and small. Her hair, in two long braids, flew out behind her. "Stop those dogs, Alex!" she said.

The man whistled. The dogs drew back.

"What you doing up there?" asked the man.

"That's no way to talk to him," said the girl. "And after this you keep those dogs tied up, or you'll be sorry."

"Yes, Miss Isabel," said the man.

The girl called to John Thomas, "You can come down now."

He climbed out of the tree. Mud and water were dripping from his clothes.

"You're hurt!" said the girl.

"No, I'm not," he said.

"Yes, you are, there on your hand," she said. "One of those dogs bit you."

He looked at his hand. "It's a scratch," he said. "I must have scratched it on the tree."

"Those dogs were still the cause of it." She said to the man, "Alex, you look after him."

"Yes, Miss Isabel." The man said to John Thomas, "Come along."

· "But I—" began John Thomas.

"Come along," said the man. "We all got to do what Miss Isabel says."

He led John Thomas to a small house back of the big house. He gave him a bath in a wooden tub. He tried to clean the mud off John Thomas' clothes.

The girl called outside the door. "Alex, come here."

The man went outside. He came back with his arms full of clothing. He said, "You can wear these till your things get dry."

He helped John Thomas into the clothes—a white linen shirt and brown homespun trousers. There were stockings and shoes, too.

John Thomas went outside. Isabel was waiting.

"You look almost like my brother," she said. "Those are his clothes."

"Will he care if I wear them?" asked John Thomas.

"He won't know it," she said. "He's away in New York. He goes to school there. Anyway, by the time he gets back, these clothes will be too little for him. I'm Isabel Hunt," she told him, "but you know that already. Are you the older boy or the younger one?"

"I—I don't know what you mean," he said.

"Aren't you one of the Simpson boys?" she asked.

"No," he said. "I'm John Thomas."

"John Thomas what?" she asked.

"Just John Thomas."

"You're *not* one of the Simpson boys?" she asked. He shook his head.

"Oh!" she said. "Oh, my goodness!"

"What's the matter?" he asked.

"There's a new family down the road," she said. "I heard there were two boys about my age. I heard they were coming here to call, and I thought you must be one of them." She asked, "Who *are* you?"

He began to tell her about himself and Half-Moon Valley. He told her about his bird and Tad Tripp, who had stolen it. "That's why I came here," he said. "I thought maybe you had seen two men and a boy go by."

"No," she said, "but maybe somebody else has. Come in, and I'll ask."

Chapter 11

The Dance

sabel's mother had not seen the Tripp brothers go by. Neither had Isabel's father.

John Thomas looked at the north road and the east road. He did not know which to take.

"Wait till your clothes dry," said Isabel. "Then make up your mind."

While he waited, she showed him the house. Never before had he seen such rooms. There were rugs on the floor and curtains at the windows. There were pictures on the walls. There were chairs and chests and tables made of dark wood that shone in the light.

60

"We have a library," said Isabel.

"What is that?" he asked.

"I'll show you." She led him into a room with shelves of books on every wall. "This is our library," she said.

He stood looking at the books.

"Have you read all these?" he asked.

"Not quite," she said.

He opened a book. "I could read this," he said. It was about a king who lived in a castle. There was a picture of the castle.

"It's a history book," said Isabel.

"Are there any books about birds?" he asked.

"Oh, yes." She showed him a large book. On almost every page were pictures of birds. They looked at the pictures together. They came to one of a crow.

"Does this look like your bird?" she asked.

"Not much," he said. "My bird is white."

"I hope you find it," she said, "and if those men won't give it back, you come here. My father will make them give it back."

"I have to find the men and the boy first," he said, "and I don't know how to find them."

"I've been thinking," she said. "There's a dance tonight. Come with us. A lot of people will be there, and you might hear something about those three brothers."

"What is a dance?" he asked.

She looked surprised. "Didn't you ever go to a dance?"

"No," he said.

"Well—it's like a party," she said, "and there's music, and the people dance."

"I never saw anyone dance," he said. "I don't know how."

"It doesn't matter," she said. "You can sit and watch. Wouldn't you like to go?"

"Yes, I would," he said.

The dance was in an old mill shed on the bank of the river. John Thomas followed Isabel and her father and mother inside. The long shed was bright with lantern light. People were standing about, laughing and talking. They spoke to Isabel and her father and mother. John Thomas felt shy among so many people.

Then the dance began, and he forgot to feel shy.

Two men played fiddles. Another played a guitar.
The sounds they made were like the wind and running water and birds singing. He said to himself,
this is music—I am hearing music!

The dancers moved about the floor as if they were flying. Sometimes they held hands and danced in a circle. Sometimes they moved back and forth. Always they kept time to the music. Never had he thought dancing would be as wonderful as this.

He and Isabel were sitting side by side. He asked her, "Do you know how to dance?"

"Oh, yes," she said.

"Is it hard to do?" he asked.

"It's easy," she said.

"Could I learn?" he asked.

"Yes," she said. "I could teach you."

A young man came over to them. He asked Isabel, "Do you want to dance with me?"

"No, thank you, Daniel," she said. "I'm with John Thomas."

He sat down beside them. He asked John Thomas, "Do you live around here?"

"No, I came from Half-Moon Valley," said John Thomas.

"He's looking for his bird," said Isabel. "It's a white crow."

"I never heard of a white crow," said Daniel.

"There aren't many in all the world," she said.

"Three brothers came to John Thomas', and one of them stole the bird."

"Three brothers?" said Daniel. "Two men and a boy?"

"Yes!" said John Thomas. "Did you see them?"

"No," said Daniel, "but my cousin did. They were down by the Pickett place, trying to buy some land."

"Did the boy have my bird?" asked John Thomas.

"My cousin didn't say," said Daniel.

"The Pickett place," said Isabel. "I know where that is."

And later, as they walked home, she told him how to get there. "Take the river trail. You'll know the house when you see it. It's made of brick."

Chapter 12

In the Stump Ground

arly in the morning John Thomas was on his way. He was wearing his deerskin clothes again. In the pocket of his shirt he could feel the corn cakes that Isabel had given him.

He came to the brick house. He knocked.

An old man opened the door.

John Thomas said, "I'm looking for the three Tripp brothers."

"They came here yesterday," said the old man. "I don't know where they went."

A little girl came up behind the old man. She

looked out at John Thomas. "I saw them this morning," she said. "They were in the stump ground."

"Where is that?" asked John Thomas.

"Across the trail and down the path," said the old man.

John Thomas found the stump ground. It was a clearing where all the trees had been cut. Only the stumps were left.

He saw no one, but he heard voices. He listened.

On the other side of the stump ground, a man came out of the woods. Behind him came another man and a boy.

They were the Tripp brothers.

They saw John Thomas. They drew close together, as if they were talking.

He went toward them.

The two men, Fred and Ernie, looked at him. The boy, Tad, looked down.

"What do you want?" asked Fred.

"I want my bird," said John Thomas.

"We haven't got it," said Fred.

"You took White Bird," John Thomas said to Tad.

"What if he did?" said Fred. "You said he could."

"No, I didn't," said John Thomas.

"He said you did," said Fred. "Anyway, it was an ugly bird. It was a hard thing to carry. It got in our way."

"Where is it?" asked John Thomas.

"We let it go," said Fred.

"But it couldn't fly," said John Thomas. "It couldn't take care of itself."

Tad spoke up. "It *could* fly—a little. It flew off —not very high, but it was flying."

Fred had started to walk away. Tad and Ernie followed him.

But Tad came back. "Down the trail about a mile, where the pine trees grow together—that's where I left the bird yesterday," he said. "They made me let it go. You might—you might still find it."

Then he ran back across the stump ground after his two brothers.

Chapter 13

Nim

ohn Thomas remembered the place where the pine trees grew close together. He walked down the trail until he found it.

"White Bird!" he called.

He went into the woods. "Bird!" he called. "White Bird!"

He came upon a little farm with a cabin and fields and rail fences. A boy was sitting on one of the fences. His clothes were ragged. His face was thin and brown.

He looked at John Thomas for a while before he spoke. "Do you live around here?"

John Thomas shook his head.

"What's your name?" asked the boy.

John Thomas told him.

"I'm Nim Timberlake," said the boy. "My father is Nim Timberlake, too. Did you come to see him?"

"No," said John Thomas. "I'm looking for my bird."

"Your what?" asked Nim.

"My bird. Somebody stole it from me and turned it loose along the trail," said John Thomas.

"What did it look like?" asked Nim.

"It's a white crow," said John Thomas. "It had a broken wing, and it couldn't fly very well. I took care of it—" He saw a strange look on Nim's face, and he asked, "Did you see my bird? Do you know anything about it?"

Nim slid down off the fence. "I saw your bird," he said.

"Where?" asked John Thomas.

"Over there, on that rock," said Nim. "It wasn't afraid of me. I knew it was somebody's pet."

John Thomas asked, "Where is it?"

"I talked to it a little," said Nim, "and I went

to the house to tell the others to come and see.
And—and—"

"And what?" asked John Thomas.

"While I was in the house," said Nim, "I heard
a shot."

John Thomas stood still.

"My big brother was out hunting," said Nim,
"and he—"

John Thomas said, "He shot my bird."

"Yes," said Nim. "He never saw anything like
it before, and he thought he had to shoot it. John
Thomas—"

"What?"

"I buried your bird," said Nim. "I buried it
under a tree. Do you want to see where?"

"No," said John Thomas.

"Do you want to come on up to the house?"
asked Nim.

John Thomas thought of the brother who had
killed White Bird. The brother might be in the
cabin. "No," he said.

"I've got a place in the woods," said Nim. "Nobody else knows about it. Come on, and I'll show
it to you."

John Thomas followed him. Nim's place was a hollow in a thicket of bushes. It was like a little room.

They lay there on the cool ground.

"Did you come a long way, looking for your bird?" asked Nim.

"Yes," said John Thomas.

"You look tired," said Nim. "You stay here and rest a while before you go home."

"I'm not going home," said John Thomas.

"Don't you have to go back to your father and mother?" asked Nim.

"I don't have any father and mother," said John Thomas. "I don't have anyone but Luke, and he let them take my bird."

"Who is Luke?" asked Nim.

John Thomas began to talk. He told about Luke and Half-Moon Valley. He told about the cradle that had floated down the river. He told about White Bird.

As he talked, he grew more and more tired. He closed his eyes. He could feel himself going to sleep.

Chapter 14

The Valley

e slept that night in Nim's place under the bushes. In the morning Nim came with breakfast—bread and meat and an ear of roasted corn.

"You can take the corn to eat on the way back," he said.

"I'm not going back," said John Thomas.

"Where *are* you going?" asked Nim.

"I don't know," said John Thomas.

"I truly wish you could stay with us. I truly do, John Thomas," said Nim, "but there's no more room in our house. The way it is now, we sleep three in a bed."

"I could stay here in the bushes," said John Thomas.

"Not when it rained. Not when it snowed," said Nim.

John Thomas thought for a while. "I'll go on to town," he said. "Maybe I could help Joe Roddy in the store."

He said good-by to Nim.

"Don't forget," said Nim. "You stop to see me the next time you're in these woods."

"I won't forget," said John Thomas.

He walked down the trail to town. He stopped at Joe Roddy's store.

"Glad to see you back," said Joe. "Did you find your bird?"

"My bird is dead," said John Thomas.

Joe said, "I'm sorry to hear that. You went to a lot of trouble to find it, too."

"Yes, I did," said John Thomas.

"Come back and sit with me," said Joe. "Rest your legs before you start on."

"I'm not going on," said John Thomas. "I thought perhaps I might stay and help you in the store."

"I'd like that," said Joe. "I'd like it fine, but the fact is, I've got all the help I need."

"Oh," said John Thomas.

"Anyway, it's best for you to get on home," said Joe. "Luke will be worrying about you."

"I don't care," said John Thomas. "He let them take my bird, and now I don't care—"

"Wait a minute," said Joe. "He let them take your bird, and you don't like that. But there must be good things about him. When you came floating down the river, who picked you up? When you were little, who fed you and took care of you?"

"He told me things that weren't so," said John Thomas. "All the things he told me about the world—they weren't so."

"Maybe they were to him," said Joe. "Maybe he sees the world one way and you see it another." He sat down beside John Thomas. "If you don't go home, where *will* you go? One of these days you can strike out and make your own way, but you're not ready yet. Can't you see you're not ready?"

John Thomas got up. He walked about the store. He took a drink from the water bucket.

Joe said, "If you want to stay here tonight and

start out in the morning, you can. But if you start now, you can get home before dark."

"I'll start now," said John Thomas.

He walked back along the river trail. He came to the hills that made a half circle about Half-Moon Valley.

He climbed the hill path. It was an old path, worn by animal feet. At the top of the hill he looked down into the valley. Evening had come. The woods and fields were in shadow.

He walked down the hill. He was nearly to the cabin when the door opened and Luke came out.

They stood looking at each other.

"So you came back," said Luke.

John Thomas said nothing.

"Where did you go?" asked Luke.

"Up the trail to find the Tripp brothers," said John Thomas.

"Did you find them?"

"Yes," said John Thomas. "My bird is dead."

"You're a sorry sight," said Luke. "All dirty and raggedy, and your hair down in your face."

"Are you going to whip me?" asked John Thomas.

"I *ought* to whip you," said Luke.

"Are you going to?" asked John Thomas.

"No." All at once Luke's voice sounded almost gone.

"Then I'll go wash." John Thomas went down to the river. He washed his hands and face.

As he sat there, a bird flew out of the willows. It looked white against the sky. He thought of White Bird and was sad.

But when he thought of White Bird, other things came to his mind. He remembered the river trail and the houses in town. He remembered Joe Roddy and Isabel and Nim. He remembered the books in the library—and the dancing—and the music. . . .

He heard footsteps. Luke had come down to the river.

"So you had to go out in the world," Luke said. "You had to go find out for yourself how it was."

John Thomas said nothing.

"You found out it was the way I said, didn't you?" said Luke.

"No," said John Thomas, "and I'm going again."

"You'll never get over that bird, will you?" said Luke. "You'll always blame me."

John Thomas sat looking at the river.

Luke said, "I did the best I could, and now you're getting ready to leave—like everybody else."

He sounded tired. He looked lonely standing there. John Thomas thought of him alone in the cabin, alone in the valley. He thought of what Joe Roddy had said: "When you came floating down the river, who picked you up? When you were little, who fed you and took care of you?"

He said, "I'm not going yet."

Luke had started up to the cabin.

John Thomas followed him. He said again, "I'm not going yet. And when I do, maybe—maybe we can *both* go. . . . Luke, didn't you hear me?"

"I heard you." Luke stopped and stood waiting for him. "Come on. It's getting dark."

ABOUT THE AUTHOR

Clyde Robert Bulla was born near King City, Missouri. He received his early education in a one-room schoolhouse, where he began writing stories and songs. After several years as a writer of magazine stories, he finished his first book, then went to work on a newspaper.

He continued to write, and his books for children became so successful that he was able to satisfy his desire to travel through the United States, Mexico, Hawaii, and Europe. He lives in Los Angeles, California.

In 1962, Mr. Bulla received the first award of the Southern California Council on Children's Literature for distinguished contributions to that field. He has written more than thirty stories for young readers.

ABOUT THE ILLUSTRATOR

Leonard Weisgard has had a wide variety of art experience. He has designed magazine covers, painted murals for Macy's, designed sets and costumes for the theatre and ballet, and illustrated innumerable books for children.

Mr. Weisgard lives in Roxbury, Connecticut, with his wife and three children. As a school board member he is active in support of school libraries, believing them to be the central core of all good schools.